COLD TURKEY

SIMON JAMES GREEN

Illustrated by
Tosin Akinkunmi

Barrington Stoke

Published by Barrington Stoke
An imprint of HarperCollins*Publishers*
1 Robroyston Gate, Glasgow, G33 1JN

www.barringtonstoke.co.uk

HarperCollins*Publishers*
Macken House, 39/40 Mayor Street Upper,
Dublin 1, DO1 C9W8, Ireland

First published in 2025

Text © 2025 Simon James Green
Illustrations © 2025 Tosin Akinkunmi
Cover design © 2025 HarperCollins*Publishers* Limited

The moral right of Simon James Green and Tosin Akinkunmi to be identified as the author and illustrator of this work has been asserted in accordance with the Copyright, Designs and Patents Act, 1988

ISBN 978-0-00-873214-1

10 9 8 7 6 5 4 3 2 1

All rights reserved. No part of this publication may be reproduced, stored in a retrieval system, or transmitted, in whole or in any part in any form or by any means, electronic, mechanical, photocopying, recording or otherwise without the prior permission in writing of the publisher and copyright owners

Without limiting the exclusive rights of any author, contributor or the publisher, any unauthorised use of this publication to train generative artificial intelligence (AI) technologies is expressly prohibited. HarperCollins also exercise their rights under Article 4(3) of the Digital Single Market Directive 2019/790 and expressly reserve this publication from the text and data mining exception

A catalogue record for this book is available from the British Library

Printed and bound in India by Replika Press Pvt. Ltd.

This book contains FSC™ certified paper and other controlled sources to ensure responsible forest management.

For more information visit: www.harpercollins.co.uk/green

For Adam Searles,
with happy memories of crazy adventures

CONTENTS

1 Cold Turkey in 2:00 hours   1

2 Cold Turkey in 1:50 hours   17

3 Cold Turkey in 1:40 hours   22

4 Cold Turkey in 1:30 hours   32

5 Cold Turkey in 1:05 hours   41

6 Cold Turkey in 50 minutes   53

7 Cold Turkey in 40 minutes   59

8 Cold Turkey in 30 minutes   66

9 Cold Turkey in 3 minutes   73

CHAPTER 1

Cold Turkey in 2:00 hours

Do you ever ask, *Why is my life so messed up?*

I do.

Picture the scene. I'm standing in Mrs Mason's flat. She's eighty years old, and she lives in the flat upstairs. Mrs Mason likes me. And I like her. She's got a hundred quid in her hands, so I like her a *lot* right now.

I lick my lips.

I'm hungry for that cash.

It's my birthday tomorrow, and that money could buy me a nice present. There's a new manga series I really want, but Mum can't afford it.

Now for the messed-up part.

On the table in front of me is a big roast turkey. I love roast turkey. It's one of my favourite things. It's sitting in front of me, golden brown, and it smells so good, begging me to eat it.

But the turkey isn't for me.

Mrs Mason wants me to deliver the turkey to her friend across town. She's got a little tartan shopping trolley for me to put the turkey in.

The trolley is *not* cool. I'm gonna look like a muppet pulling it along.

But Mrs Mason doesn't care about that. She wants me to pull a turkey in a trolley from south to north London. It's going to take me an hour to get to her friend's house.

Like, can't she just do it herself?

But it's even more messed up than that.

She wants Hamza to help me.

Hamza is here too. He's next to me. He's also looking at the cash and licking his lips.

Hamza lives in the flat next door to me. We also go to the same school. We have zero rizz, and everyone picks on us. You stick together when nobody likes you. When we're not at school, we spend a lot of time on Hamza's PlayStation playing *Afterlife 5*. It's a game where you work together to protect yourself from a mob of killer zombies. Which is exactly like school is for us. That's probably why we're so good at it.

Hamza is my best mate.

Correction: he *was* my best mate.

Now he's my worst enemy.

I found out that Hamza is a lying, cheating no-good thief, and I want nothing more to do with him.

"So, how about it, boys?" Mrs Mason says. She's still got that wodge of cash in her hand. "One hundred pounds," she says. "That's fifty pounds each. If you deliver this turkey to my friend Maggie."

I don't know what to do. I want the money. But I do not want to do this job with Hamza. "I dunno," I say.

Mrs Mason doesn't understand. "I thought you and Hamza liked doing odd jobs for money?" she says to me.

I nod and say, "Uh-huh."

"So what's the problem?" Mrs Mason asks me.

"I don't want to work with him any more," I say.

Mrs Mason frowns. She says, "Why not?"

"Because Hamza stole all of last month's profits," I tell her.

"That's not true!" Hamza pipes up.

I glare at him.

"OK, it's a bit true," he admits.

I glare at him some more.

"OK, it's mostly true," he says. He smiles at Mrs Mason. "I need to chat with the Bossman in private," he says.

He's trying to be nice. He thinks if he calls me "the Bossman" I'll like him again. I won't. I washed cars for that money. I mowed lawns. I even unblocked someone's toilet. I'm proper angry with Hamza.

Mrs Mason frowns, but she does what Hamza asked. She goes out so it's just Hamza and me. And the roast turkey.

"Kit," Hamza says – Kit's my real name. "Kit, look, I'm sorry I took the money, OK?"

"No, it's not OK!" I say. "It was fifty quid! You should have asked me!"

"I ... couldn't," he says. "I felt stupid."

I don't understand. I ask him, "Why's that?"

Hamza looks embarrassed. "I bought Tiffany Dior some flowers with the money."

"Why did you do that?" I ask.

Hamza frowns. He says, "She's special. Tiffany Dior is the nicest and most beautiful girl in the school!"

"But why did you buy her flowers?"

"So she'd go out with me," Hamza replies.

"And did she?"

"No," Hamza says. "She told me to come back when my balls dropped."

I laugh. I can't help it.

"It's not funny!" Hamza moans. "It's not OK to talk about my balls, man. That's private!" He tuts.

"Is that why you weren't free to play *Afterlife 5* last week? Because you were busy taking flowers to Tiffany Dior?"

"Yes," Hamza mutters, not looking at me.

"I can't believe it! You stole money from me to buy flowers for a girl, and you put her before *Afterlife 5*? What sort of mate are you?" I ask.

"I'm sorry, man." Hamza shoves his hands into the pockets of his shorts and scuffs his Crocs on the floor. "Look, if we do this job," he says, "I'll pay you back out of my half. How about that?"

I think about it. I do want the money. And I'll only have to spend an hour or so with Hamza. I'll get more than fifty quid when it's over. I can do that. "OK, fine," I say.

Hamza smiles. "You'll do it?"

"Yes."

"Wicked!" Hamza says, and snaps his fingers.

"But we're still not mates!" I say.

"I promise I won't even speak to you," Hamza says.

"Good!"

"I promise I won't even look at you!" Hamza goes on.

"Good!"

"I promise if you catch on fire, I won't even pee on you to put it out," Hamza tells me.

I stare at him.

"Unless you want me to?" he asks when I don't say anything.

"No, Hamza, I do not want you to pee on me!" I say.

"Even if you're on fire?" he asks.

"Why would I be on fire?"

Hamza shrugs. "I dunno, bro, stuff happens. I heard about this woman once – just a normal day, and she randomly exploded in flames."

"You said you weren't going to talk to me, so now's a good time to shut up," I say.

"Sure," Hamza replies. "We're just two people who hate each other, taking a turkey across London for an old lady. What could go wrong?"

I sigh. Like I told you before, my life is so messed up.

"Hey, Mrs Mason?" Hamza shouts. "Wrap that turkey in silver foil! We're on, baby!"

CHAPTER 2

Cold Turkey in 1:50 hours

Hamza wants to pull the trolley. Maybe he thinks it gives him extra rizz. That's how clueless he is. He's pulling the trolley as we walk down the high street. I want to get this over with as fast as possible.

"Hurry up!" I tell him.

"Chill!" Hamza tells me. "Mrs Mason said the turkey will stay hot for two hours. It only takes one hour to get to Maggie's house, so we've got plenty of time!"

"You said you weren't going to talk," I huff.

"You started chatting first!" he says.

It annoys me that he's right. I promise myself that I won't say anything else to him.

"Mmmm!" Hamza says, breathing in. "It sure smells good though! I love turkey! I mean, I love chicken more. Especially fried chicken. That special blend of secret spices ..."

"Stop talking about food!" I snap.

"Why? Are you hungry too?" Hamza asks. "Hungry for some tasty fried chicken? And maybe some fries ... and perhaps a side of beans?"

"Or that nice gravy they do?" I say.

"Yeah, or the corn ..." Hamza adds.

Ahh, man, I can almost taste it. But then I snap out of it. "No! Let's just get this done!"

Hamza looks over at the shop to our right. "We're just outside Chicken Lickin' though," he says.

Chicken Lickin' is our favourite chicken shop. Hamza and I have spent many a happy time in that shop. But it feels wrong to go in there now, when I hate Hamza so much.

"And look!" Hamza says. "They have a deal on! Two meals for the price of one!"

That is an amazing deal.

And I am very hungry.

It's also true that we have plenty of time. Also, Mrs Mason gave us half the cash up front, so we also have money to spend.

"Fine, let's eat," I say.

"Yay!" Hamza says.

"At separate tables!" I add. "Because I hate you."

He smiles and blows me a kiss. He's so annoying I want to scream.

CHAPTER 3

Cold Turkey in 1:40 hours

The chicken shop is so full that Hamza and I have to sit at the same table. Fine! That still doesn't mean we're mates. I'm just gonna ignore him.

I grab the tray of food from the counter and take it to the only table that's free, while Hamza pulls the trolley and tucks it behind his seat. Behind him, an elderly lady and her friend are eating chicken burgers. To the side, a family has a bargain bucket. Everyone is chatting. Everyone is having a good time.

Everyone except me and Hamza.

"You could just talk to me," Hamza says, dipping a fry in gravy.

"I don't wanna talk," I tell him.

"I messed up," Hamza says. "I admit it! Just give me a second chance."

"It isn't just about the money," I say. "What if you had actually gone out with Tiffany? I bet I'd never see you again! There'd be no more *Afterlife 5* gaming sessions because you'd be too busy sticking your tongue down Tiffany's throat!"

"No!" Hamza says. "Me and you? We're a team. We look out for each other! Always will!"

"Not any more," I say.

We don't say anything else. We sit and eat our food. I almost feel bad, but then I remember he stole my half of the money. A friend wouldn't do that.

I see the elderly lady has got up from the table behind Hamza and is pulling her shopping trolley behind her towards the exit. Her trolley looks exactly like ours.

I suddenly panic. "Where's our trolley, Hamza?" I ask.

"Chill," he says. "It's right here."

I could have sworn he put it at the other side of his chair, but maybe I was wrong. It would be a good idea to check.

"Hamza!" I say.

"I am eating chicken," he replies.

"Yeah, but, Hamza—"

"Do not spoil how much I'm loving the secret spice mix," he tells me.

"No, but, Hamza! Seriously! You need to check that's our trolley!" I insist.

"Bro, it's our trolley," he says.

"Bro, that lady has the exact same trolley!" I reply.

Hamza shakes his head and twists around in his seat. "Whatever," he says as he lifts up the lid of the trolley. He peers inside and frowns. "Kit, did you put five packets of fig rolls and a tin of Spam in here?"

"No," I say.

"Oh crap, this isn't our trolley!" Hamza says.

"That lady took the wrong trolley!" I squeal.

We're out of there as fast as we can run, onto the busy street. I look left. Hamza looks right. Where is she? "Down there!" I say, spotting the old lady about twenty metres down the pavement. "Stop!" I shout as we run towards her. "Lady? Please stop!"

She does not stop.

"I don't think she can hear us!" I say.

"Idea!" Hamza says. "STOP THIEF!" he screams.

I slap myself on the head. "You can't say that, Hamza!" I groan. "She took our trolley by mistake!"

"How d'you know?" Hamza says. "She might pull this trick all the time. She looks well sus."

The woman still doesn't stop. And no one else is helping. They're just staring at us like we're weird.

Hamza looks hard at me. "Right!" he says.

Before I can stop him, he sprints off towards the lady and tries to rugby tackle her to the ground. He misses. Instead, he falls over and skids along the pavement. It looks painful. But good news: he's blocked her. And the trolley's not going anywhere.

A group of people stop to see what's going on.

One of them is a policeman.

CHAPTER 4

Cold Turkey in 1:30 hours

Everyone is shouting.

"That boy tried to mug this old lady!" a man says, pointing at Hamza.

"Lies!" Hamza replies. "That old lady stole *our* trolley!"

"This is my trolley!" the old lady says.

Then the old lady stamps on Hamza's foot.

"OWW!" he screams. "Why did you do that?"

"Because you're a no-good liar!" the old lady replies.

Everyone's yelling and shoving. It takes about ten minutes for Hamza and me to explain. Even then, the policeman doesn't believe us.

"It's very odd to be taking a roast turkey across London," he says.

"We're helping out an old lady," Hamza says.

"There are a lot of old ladies in your life," the policeman says.

Hamza shrugs. "We're good boys who like helping people, that's all," he says.

I give him the side-eye. There's nothing "good" about Hamza.

At last, we get the other trolley from the chicken shop, the old lady sees she's made a mistake and everyone calms down.

Everyone except Hamza. He's looking at his phone as we walk along. "We've only got an hour and twenty minutes left!" he says.

"We've got to get moving!" I tell him.

"It'll be OK," Hamza says. "There's a Tube station at the end of this street. That'll take us up to Maggie's house in about half an hour."

That sounds like a plan. But when we get to the station, there's a sign up which reads: "Long delays".

I groan.

"Come on!" Hamza says. "We'll just have to hope a train comes quickly."

We go through the ticket barriers and hurry down to the platform.

For once in our lives, we're lucky! There's a train waiting!

We give each other a high five. We've *so* got this.

"Stand clear!" someone says over the loudspeaker. "This train is ready to depart!"

"Quick!" Hamza shouts. "We don't want to miss it!"

Hamza runs towards the train. He lifts the shopping trolley onto the train first but then jumps back as the doors suddenly snap shut.

The trolley is on the train.

Hamza and I are still on the platform.

Hamza jabs at the button to make the doors open.

But the doors won't open.

Then the train leaves.

"No, no, no, no, no!" Hamza says as the train vanishes into the tunnel.

"You had one job!" I tell him. "All you had to do was keep the turkey safe, and you couldn't even do that!" I'm so angry. But there's no time for that now. We need to get the turkey back.

"We need to get to the next station," Hamza says. "With all the delays, it'll be quicker to run there. If I tell a member of staff, they should be able to get the trolley off the train and have it waiting for us."

"Promise you won't mess this up again?"

"I promise," Hamza tells me.

CHAPTER 5

Cold Turkey in 1:05 hours

I close my eyes and try to stay calm while Hamza goes to speak to a staff member. Then we run to the next underground station. It takes us ages because Hamza's limping after the old lady stamped on his foot, and I'm wearing socks and sliders, and it's pretty hard to run.

We're hot and sweaty. We're breathless. I'm panting so hard I suck up a fly by accident.

I am so over today, and I am so over Hamza. All of this is his fault.

We round the corner, and we stop dead.

There are loads of police cars outside the station.

The road has been taped off.

There are police everywhere.

And a van with the words "Bomb Squad" written on the side.

I hear one of the police officers say, "There's a suspected bomb on one of the trains!"

I have a very bad feeling. I turn to Hamza. "What *exactly* did you say to the staff member at the last station?" I ask him.

"I told them we'd left our trolley on the train, and we had to get it back," Hamza says.

"Those were your exact words?" I say.

"More or less," he says. "I was in a rush. I can't remember clearly."

"What *exactly* did you say, Hamza?" I ask him again. "Think hard."

Hamza takes a breath. "I said ... there's a trolley on the train ... and we need it back, else ... BOOM!"

I stare at him. "Boom?"

"Yeah," Hamza says. "Like, we'll be in so much trouble our world will explode!"

"Explode?" I say. "Like a bomb?"

"Exactly like a bomb!" Hamza says with a grin. Then he sees the Bomb Squad van. "Uh-oh. Maybe they didn't understand!"

"Oh, you think?" I say.

"They think there's a real bomb in the trolley!" Hamza says.

One of the police officers shouts, "Stand back, everyone!" A little robot truck comes out from the station. It's pushing our trolley out into the road.

"We're going to destroy the trolley!" shouts a policeman. "Clear the area!"

"Why are they going to destroy it?" Hamza asks me.

"Because they think there's a bomb inside it!" I reply.

"Only a fool would think that!" Hamza says.

"There's only one fool around here, and that's you!" I scream at him.

My screaming makes all the police turn around and look at us. One of them walks over. She's a tall woman. She looks very cross and very serious. "You boys should not be here," she says. "It's very dangerous."

"That's our trolley!" I tell her.

"It's got a bomb in it," she says.

"No, it hasn't. It's got a turkey in it," I reply.

The policewoman looks puzzled. She goes to speak to another policeman.

The policeman approaches the trolley and carefully looks inside. "Smells like roast turkey!" he says.

The policewoman comes back over. "Who is the young man who said there was a bomb inside the trolley?" she asks. "Because he is in a lot of trouble."

I turn to look at Hamza, but he's not there. He's run off.

I know why.

Hamza's always in trouble at school.

Everyone thinks he's useless. His parents as well.

He really doesn't want to get in trouble with the police because then all those people will think they were right about him. I feel sorry for him even though I'm still really angry. I can't explain it.

I look back at the policewoman. My mouth is very dry because I'm so nervous. But I'm gonna do it. I'm gonna take the bullet for Hamza.

"It was me," I lie. "It was me who said about the trolley being a bomb. But I didn't mean it – not how it came out anyway."

It's not as easy as that, of course. I have to speak to some other police officers too. Some stuff gets written down and everyone looks like they hate me.

In the end, they hand the trolley back.

I wheel it around the corner, away from the station. Hamza is waiting on a bench.

"Am I under arrest?" he asks. He looks really sad.

I shake my head. "I sorted it."

"You took the blame?" he asks.

I nod.

"Why did you do that?"

I shrug. "Dunno," I say.

"Is it because we're mates again?" He looks at me hopefully.

"No, Hamza, we are not!" I say. "It was just the best way to sort this out." I look at the time on my phone. "Ahh, man. Now we've only got fifty minutes before the turkey gets cold."

"Should we try to take another Tube train?" Hamza asks.

"We can't. They've banned me from the whole network," I say.

"Huh," Hamza says. "That sucks. OK, don't worry. I have another plan."

I groan.

"No, it's fine," he continues. "This time, nothing can go wrong."

CHAPTER 6

Cold Turkey in 50 minutes

The plan is to take a shortcut.

Hamza knows the way. He says his uncle had a shop around here, and he spent a lot of time in the area when he was younger.

"Down here," Hamza says. He's pointing to an alleyway. There's a fence down one side and the wall of an old factory down the other side. The windows are boarded up. There's broken glass on the ground. Graffiti on the walls. This is not a good place. It doesn't feel safe.

Hamza must know how I'm feeling because he says, "I promise it'll be quicker if we go down here."

Maybe. But I'm still not sure.

"Hey, I know it looks like something from a horror movie," Hamza says, "but this alleyway is safe. Back in the day, I was here all the time. Trust me. And don't be chicken."

"I'm not chicken," I tell him.

"BWARK!" he replies.

"I'm not chicken ... but I'm also not an idiot. This is the sort of place people get mugged!" I say.

"BWARK!"

"Right, OK, let's just do it," I say.

We start to walk down the alleyway.

Am I being chicken? The alleyway seems to get darker as we go down it. And colder. It feels as if the wall and the fence are closing in on us ... trapping us ...

"See, it's fine!" Hamza says. "Look, there's even some nice people up ahead!"

I look at the three lads standing at the end of the alley.

They're all wearing masks. And hoodies. And they're watching us.

In a panic, I turn around, looking for an escape. But there, right behind us, are two more lads. They're also wearing masks and hoodies.

They're ahead of us. They're behind us. There's a wall on one side. There's a fence on the other side. We've walked right into a trap.

"Hamza …" I say nervously.

"Oops," Hamza says. "This may have been a mistake."

One of the gang steps forward. He's the tallest. I can only see his eyes – and they're cold and mean. "You bet it was a mistake," he says.

CHAPTER 7

Cold Turkey in 40 minutes

The gang march us down the alley.

"Ow!" Hamza says. "Stop being so rough!"

"You're on our turf!" says the tall lad with mean eyes.

They push us through the door of the old factory. When we get inside, I'm surprised. It's a big empty room with a concrete floor.

But in the corner they've got a big rug and a sofa. They've also set up a gaming area with a huge TV screen. There's a fridge and even a popcorn machine.

"Cool," I say.

"Shut it!" says the tall lad. "What are your names?"

"Batman and Robin," Hamza replies.

The tall lad stares at him. He says, "Any more of your crap, and you're dead meat."

Hamza mimes zipping his mouth shut.

"I'm Kit and he's Hazma," I say.

"I'm Spike," the lad replies. "What's in the trolley? Is it drugs?"

"Drugs?" Hamza says. "You mean, like Lemsip?"

"*Hard* drugs," Spike replies.

"Ohh!" Hamza says. "Lemsip Max!"

"It's a turkey, if you must know," I say quickly.

The smallest gang member with a baseball cap says, "I love turkey!"

"Well, how about that?" Spike says. "Frankie here loves turkey. Looks like it's your lucky day, Frankie-boy, cos these lads have just delivered your favourite food!"

"You can't have the turkey," Hamza says.

"We can have whatever we want," Spike replies. He grabs hold of the trolley.

"No!" Hamza says. "Anything but that! Have something else! Have my Crocs!"

"Why would I want your skanky old Crocs?" Spike says.

I watch Hamza's face as he tries to think of something else he can trade for the turkey. His eyes search the room ... and settle on the big TV screen and gaming console. "You got *Afterlife 5*?"

"What if we have?" Spike says.

Hamza smiles. "How about a challenge? Kit and me against you and Frankie. If you win, you can keep the turkey. If we win, we get the turkey, and you set us free."

"One thing though," Spike says.

"Anything!" Hamza replies.

"We play on the hardest level."

Hamza gulps, and my heart starts to beat fast. Hamza and I have never played the hardest level before. We're not good enough.

"Deal!" Hamza says.

I feel myself die inside.

CHAPTER 8

Cold Turkey in 30 minutes

Me and Hamza are playing as humans. Spike and Frankie are playing as zombies. The game starts, and it's a total nightmare. Spike and Frankie are *so* good. They chase us. They fire at us. In just one minute, we're bleeding and losing points.

Hamza and I have never played this level before. We don't know where anything is.

Even worse, when we play at Hamza's, we talk to each other as we go along. We tell each other what to do. But we can't do that here. Spike and Frankie are right next to us. If we say anything, they'll know what we're planning.

Two minutes later, and they've got us. Spike and Frankie's zombies have trapped us in a room with only one exit. They've got guns and a missile launcher. I've only got two grenades left. Hamza has nothing. The odds are not good.

But I know what Hamza's gonna do.

He's my best mate – of course I know.

He's gonna do what he's done every single time today.

He's gonna do what he always does.

He's gonna do the stupidest thing possible. He's gonna take a deep breath, close his eyes and hope he'll beat the odds.

He's gonna run towards that door.

He's gonna run towards two zombies who have guns, grenades AND missile launchers.

It's a move no one in their right mind would make.

It's certain death.

But that's exactly what he does.

I don't think Spike or Frankie can believe he's just running towards them. They laugh. They think they've got this in the bag because they have so many weapons and he has nothing. But I'm ready. That laughter gives me a chance to hurl my grenades.

BOOM! BOOM!

Two direct hits!

Two dead zombies.

And thanks to Hamza's crazy-ass stupidity, and thanks to me knowing my mate really well …

We've won.

The gang are all in shock as Hamza and I grab the trolley and swagger out of there.

The minute we're outside, we run.

And we don't stop until we're streets away.

Then we flop down laughing.

"How did you know I was gonna pull that move at the end?" Hamza asks.

I look at him and shake my head. "I just asked myself, *What would a normal, sane person do?* And I knew you'd do the opposite," I say.

"Brilliant!" Hamza tells me.

We have to get going. We only have fifteen minutes left before the turkey will be cold. We hurry along the streets until we get to Maggie's house.

We have three minutes to go when we arrive. I ring the doorbell. "Come on, come on!" I say.

An elderly lady with grey hair answers the door. "Ahh, Kit and Hamza? I've been expecting you!" she says. "In you come!"

We walk inside. It's a nice house. It's old with high ceilings. I pull the trolley into the kitchen and …

CHAPTER 9

Cold Turkey in 3 minutes

"SURPRISE!" Hamza, Maggie and Mrs Mason all shout.

The kitchen has been decorated with balloons and streamers. There's a pile of presents on the table. And on the work surfaces there are roast potatoes, carrots, pigs in blankets and a big jug of gravy. *What the hell is going on?*

"Happy birthday for tomorrow, Kit!" Mrs Mason says. "Welcome to your birthday lunch!"

"Huh?" I mutter. I'm totally confused.

"I heard all about you and Hamza falling out," Mrs Mason says. "So I planned this for you. I thought that maybe if you had to spend some time together, you'd sort it all out."

"I agreed it was worth a go," Hamza adds.

"You were in on this?" I squeal.

Hamza nods. "Yeah. Although I didn't think the trip would be so stressful."

I'm so shocked I can hardly speak. "This is all ... for me?"

"I wanted to show you that I was sorry about taking the money," Hamza says. "Also, even if Tiffany had gone out with me, there's no way she'd have stuck by my side like you did today. Tiffany's nice ... but you're awesome."

"So are you, mate," I tell him. "We're a good team."

"I agree," Hamza says. "I know other people think we're weird. I know they say we're losers. And I know I get us into a stupid mess sometimes. But at least we have each other!"

"And there's no one else I would rather be in a stupid mess with!" I say.

Hamza smiles. "Mates?" he asks.

"Mates!" I say.

We give each other a hug. It feels good to have him back.

Maggie has got the turkey out. "It's perfect – and still hot!" she says.

"Come on then," I say. "Let's eat!"

I give Hamza a fist bump. And I understand something in that moment. Today has been full of ups and downs. Just like life is always full of ups and downs. There are amazing bits, and there are bad bits. Sometimes, there are *really* bad bits. And that's when you ask yourself, *Why is my life so messed up?*

But know what? When you've got a good mate by your side, you can face that mess together. And maybe life isn't perfect, but it sure feels a little bit better.

Our books are tested
for children and young people by
children and young people.

Thanks to everyone who consulted on
a manuscript for their time and effort in
helping us to make our books better
for our readers.